Lucy
the Diamond
Fairy

To Holly Caitlin Powell,
with lots of love

Special thanks to
Sue Mongredien

No part of this publication may be reproduced, stored in a retrieval system, or transmitted in any form or by any means, electronic, mechanical, photocopying, recording, or otherwise, without written permission of the publisher. For information regarding permission, write to Rainbow Magic Limited c/o HIT Entertainment, 830 South Greenville Avenue, Allen, TX 75002-3320.

ISBN-13: 978-0-545-01194-5
ISBN-10: 0-545-01194-9

12 11   16/0

Printed in the U.S.A.   40

First Scholastic printing, January 2008

Lucy
the Diamond
Fairy

by Daisy Meadows

illustrated by Georgie Ripper

LITTLE · APPLE

SCHOLASTIC INC.

New York   Toronto   London   Auckland   Sydney
Mexico City   New Delhi   Hong Kong   Buenos Aires

The Fairyland Palace

Adventure Playground

Tippington Manor

Tippington Town

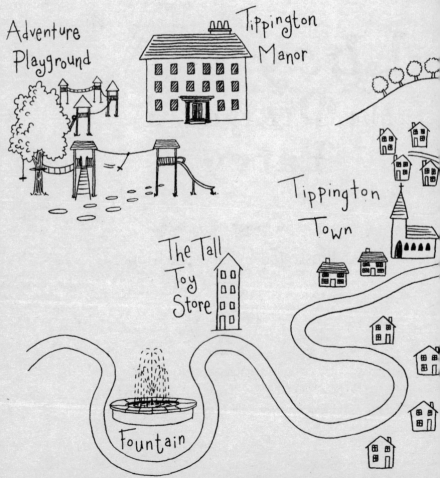

The Tall Toy Store

Fountain

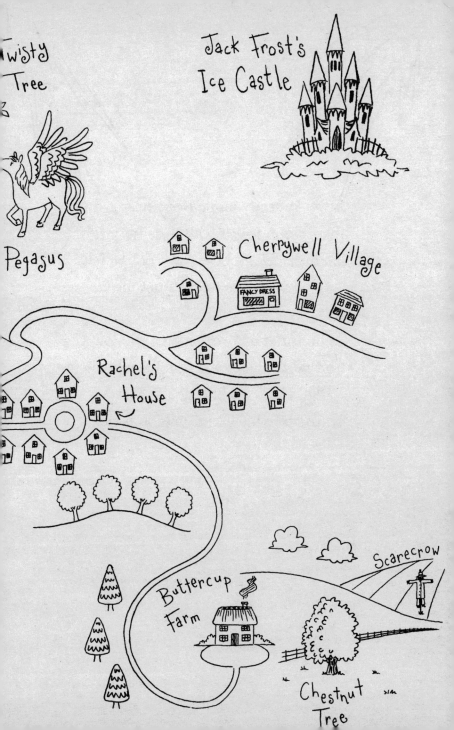

By frosty magic I cast away
These seven jewels with their fiery rays,
So their magic powers will not be felt
And my icy castle shall not melt.

The fairies may search high and low
To find the gems and take them home.
But I will send my goblin guards
To make the fairies' mission hard.

Contents

Off to Fairyland!

Kirsty Tate folded her sweatshirt and put it into her bag. "There," she said to her best friend, Rachel Walker. "I'm all packed." She looked at the clock on Rachel's bedroom wall. "Six o'clock already!" Kirsty groaned. "Mom and Dad will be here to pick me up soon. I can't believe this week is almost over, can you?"

1

Rachel shook her head. "No," she replied. "It's gone so fast! But it's been a lot of fun."

The girls grinned at each other. Whenever they were together, the two of them always had the most wonderful adventures: fairy adventures! This week, the girls had been helping the Jewel Fairies find the seven magic jewels missing from Fairy Queen Titania's crown.

Mean Jack Frost had stolen the gems. Without them, some very important kinds of fairy magic were running low. So far, Kirsty and Rachel had found six of the stolen jewels — but the diamond was still missing.

Kirsty frowned. "I can't help feeling like something's wrong today," she said.

"I was sure we'd find the magic diamond before I had to go home."

"Me, too," Rachel agreed. "And we haven't seen a fairy today, either. I wonder if they're all trapped in Fairyland?"

The girls exchanged worried glances. They both knew that the diamond controlled flying magic. Because it was missing, the fairies were starting to lose their ability to fly.

The last fairy the girls had seen, Sophie the Sapphire Fairy, had fading wings.

"We'll just have to find the diamond and send it back to Fairyland ourselves,"

Kirsty said in a determined voice. "Do you think we should start looking now?"

Before Rachel could reply, both girls gasped in surprise.

"Kirsty, your locket is glowing!" Rachel cried.

"So is yours!" Kirsty's eyes widened in surprise. "I think I know what this means . . ."

". . . Our fairy friends need us!" Rachel finished.

The Fairy King and Queen had given each girl a locket filled with magic fairy dust. Just a pinch of fairy

dust would whisk them away to
Fairyland! Last time the king and queen
needed their help, when the seven jewels
were first stolen, Rachel's and Kirsty's
lockets also glowed. But why would they
go to Fairyland now? There was still one
jewel left to find!

Rachel's eyes were wide. "What if
the diamond isn't here? What if it's in
Fairyland, and that's why the king and

queen are calling us?" she wondered
out loud.

Kirsty nodded and quickly opened her
locket. "Let's use our last pinches of fairy
dust to get there," she suggested.

"Good idea," Rachel
agreed. "Let's go!"

Both girls sprinkled the
glittering golden dust
over themselves.
Whoosh! Everything
blurred into a whirlwind
of sparkling rainbow
colors. The girls felt
like they were
tumbling through the
air, shrinking smaller
and smaller as
they spun.

Moments later, they found themselves
landing gently at the foot of a tall,
twisting tree. It stretched high above their
heads. In front of them stood King
Oberon and Queen Titania, with all
seven of the Jewel Fairies.

"We're back in Fairyland," Kirsty
cheered, "and we're fairy-size!" She

flapped her shimmering wings happily. Being a fairy was so much fun!

"Welcome back, girls," King Oberon said warmly.

"Hello," Rachel replied, smiling. She saw that almost all of the magical jewels were back in the queen's crown, glittering brightly in the sun. But Rachel's smile faded as she suddenly realized that something was terribly wrong. "Your Majesties!" she gasped, looking around. "Where are all the fairies' wings?"

starlight, starbright

Queen Titania sighed sadly. "Thank you for coming, Kirsty and Rachel," she said. "As you can see, we don't have any of the diamond's magic power left. Our wings all grew fainter and fainter, and now they have disappeared. None of us can fly!"

Kirsty's own wings trembled as she

heard this shocking news. "But . . .
but . . . *we* have wings." She pointed up,
confused.

King Oberon nodded. "That's because
you just used your fairy dust. Its magic is
still strong, but it won't last very long."

A fairy with short golden hair
stepped forward. She was wearing
a white top and skirt, decorated with

ice-blue diamonds that
sparkled whenever she
moved. The girls knew
that she must be Lucy
the Diamond Fairy!
"We think the
diamond is up in
the Twisty Tree,"
she told the girls,
pointing to the

towering tree beside them. "We spotted four goblins here earlier today. Goblins never come into Fairyland unless they're causing trouble!"

"Do you think they were looking for the diamond?" Rachel asked.

Lucy nodded. "They spent a long time

arguing over who should climb the Twisty Tree to guard the diamond," she went on. Her eyes twinkled. "But this is the tallest tree in Fairyland, and goblins don't like heights. After hours of fighting about it, they all decided to come back tomorrow, instead."

"So what should we do?" Kirsty asked, gazing up at the tree. It really was tall, she realized. Its knotty trunk stretched up beyond the clouds and out of sight.

Lucy hesitated. "Well, I'd fly up and look for the diamond myself, but . . ." She looked over her shoulder at the spot where her wings used to be. "I can't," she finished sadly.

"Well, then, Rachel and I will fly up there and find the diamond for you!" Kirsty declared.

Lucy clapped her hands. "Oh, I was hoping you'd say that," she cried.

"Thank you, girls," the queen added. "But please be very careful."

"We will," Rachel promised. "Come on, Kirsty. Let's go!"

The girls flapped their wings and headed up the Twisty Tree, while the Fairy King and Queen headed back to their palace. The tree trunk was thick and gnarled, and a tangle of branches stretched out in all different directions. Kirsty and Rachel searched along every branch, carefully peeking under all the leaves and into all the white flowers. The girls knew that Jack Frost had wanted to keep the seven magic jewels for himself, but he had thrown them away when he'd realized they were too hot to keep in his ice palace. Even though the other jewels ended up in the human world, it seemed that the diamond had hidden itself in Fairyland! Up and up the girls went. Soon they had flown right through the fluffy Fairyland clouds! "I've seen lots of bluebirds and hundreds of silver butterflies," Rachel said after a while. "But no diamond!" "Me, too," Kirsty called from higher up. "But Lucy seemed sure that it was here somewhere."

The girls continued their search, hoping to see a familiar sparkle. Eventually, they found themselves at the very top of the

tree — but they still hadn't seen any sign of the diamond!

"Do you think we missed it?" Kirsty asked.

"I don't think so," Rachel replied, disappointed. "We were looking so carefully." She shrugged. "We'd better fly back down and tell Lucy we couldn't find it, before *our* wings disappear, too."

"I guess so." Kirsty sighed.

The sun was setting, and the sky above Fairyland was turning from a beautiful pink to a deep red. Before Kirsty and Rachel had gotten very far down the tree, the sky had darkened further to a purply-blue.

17

"Look," Rachel said, hovering in midair as she gazed around. "Fairyland stars. Aren't they pretty?"

Kirsty watched as the twinkling lights appeared in the dark sky. "They're beautiful," she breathed.

"Look at that one," Rachel said, pointing off into the distance. "It's really bright!"

Kirsty turned to look. The star was bigger and brighter than anything else in the sky. "It's different from the others," she remarked. "It looks almost magical. . . ."

Both girls gasped as the same thought hit them.

"The magic diamond!" Kirsty cried.

"It's hidden in the sky with the stars!" Rachel finished.

A Frosty Encounter

Both girls zoomed toward the glittering diamond, which shone bright white in the velvety blue darkness. Kirsty noticed that this jewel was smaller than the others she and Rachel had found. In the human world, the gems had been as big as eggs. But here in Fairyland, the diamond was fairy-size. It was no bigger

than an apple seed — but it seemed
bigger now that Rachel and Kirsty were
fairy-size, too.

Kirsty stretched out her hand to grab
the jewel as she got closer to it. But just
before her fingers touched it, an icy wind
sprang up out of nowhere. The wind
blew Kirsty and Rachel away from
the diamond!

"Help!" Kirsty cried as the wind sent both girls tumbling through the sky. They couldn't fly at all! Luckily, they were swept back into the Twisty Tree. They clung gratefully to the branches as the wind howled around them.

"Where did this storm come from?" Kirsty shivered, huddling closer to Rachel.

Rachel frowned as the wind moaned through the branches. "It feels like a magic storm," she said. "I wonder —"

But before Rachel could finish her sentence, both girls heard a nasty laugh. "Jack Frost!" gasped Kirsty as a dark, spiky figure zoomed toward them on a wintry blast of air. Jack Frost sneered at the girls. "Trying to reach the diamond?" he said. "Well, you'll never get it. You aren't strong enough to fly in my

24

ice storm!" With that, Jack Frost pointed his glittering wand to the sky and sent an icy lightning bolt hurtling toward the girls!

The lightning crackled as it shot through the air. Rachel and Kirsty threw themselves out of the way just in time. The ice bolt struck the tree trunk nearby, and frost crystals glittered all around it.

"Hurry!" Kirsty hissed. "We can't fly, but we can climb back down the tree. Come on!"

Rachel followed her friend. "We'll have to tell Lucy what happened," she said, clambering down the tree trunk as quickly as she could.

"And we need to think of a way to get the diamond away from that horrible Jack Frost," Kirsty added in a low voice, climbing down through the clouds.

The fluffy layer of clouds seemed to be shielding the air below from Jack Frost's storm. As Kirsty and Rachel emerged from underneath it, they were relieved to find that the air was calmer. The girls could fly the rest of the way to the ground.

Lucy was waiting for them there. "Are you all right?" she asked.

Kirsty quickly told her what had

happened. Lucy cheered when she heard that they'd found the diamond. But then, when Kirsty told her that Jack Frost was guarding the jewel, Lucy groaned.

"Jack Frost is much harder to trick than his goblins," she said, frowning.

"So what can we do?" Rachel asked.

"Maybe if Rachel and I distract Jack Frost," Kirsty said slowly, "somebody else could sneak up and grab the diamond while he isn't looking. It's too bad we don't have any fairy dust left. Lucy, is there *any* fairy who is still strong enough to fly?"

Lucy shook her head sadly. The three friends fell silent, trying to think of a new plan to rescue the diamond.

Then, suddenly, a smile appeared
on Lucy's face. She started dancing up
and down. "That's it! Of course!"
she laughed. "Kirsty — you're
a genius!"

Fairy Friends to the Rescue

"I am?" Kirsty replied, looking surprised.

"Yes — because Pegasus will help us!" Lucy cried. She grinned at the girls' blank expressions. "He's a winged horse who lives right here in Fairyland. He's wonderful! I'll see if I can use a spell to call him."

Kirsty's and Rachel's eyes widened. Pegasus! They waited excitedly as Lucy waved her wand, sending ice-white sparkles spiraling into the air. Suddenly, the girls felt a strong wind swirl around them. They looked nervously up at the sky, afraid that they'd see Jack Frost flying toward them. But then both girls gasped in delight. There, beating his great, feathered wings, was a silvery-white flying horse!

Pegasus whinnied softly as he landed next to Lucy and nuzzled her shoulder.

The little fairy stroked his silky white mane. "Oh, Pegasus, thank you for coming," she said. "We need your help!"

As Lucy told Pegasus what was going on, Kirsty and Rachel both realized that they couldn't take their eyes off the winged horse. His mane and tail sparkled in the starlight, and his body seemed to glow with a magical white light.

Pegasus nodded his great head and stamped a hoof. "He'll do it!" Lucy cried, and threw her arms around his neck. "I knew he'd help!" She beamed at the girls as she climbed onto Pegasus's back.

"While you two distract Jack Frost, Pegasus and I will fly up behind him and get the diamond," Lucy declared.

"Hooray!" cried Kirsty. "Let's go!"

Kirsty, Rachel, and Pegasus all flapped their wings and flew up into the dark night sky. Lucy waved her wand, sending a stream of sparkling white stars ahead to light their way.

Kirsty and Rachel looked nervously
at each other as they got closer to the
diamond. "Come on," Kirsty said,
grabbing Rachel's hand. "We can do
this. We have to — the fairies need
our help!"

The two friends kept flying, trying
to be brave. Here above the clouds,
the air was cold but calm again.
Jack Frost's storm had stopped.

"There's Jack Frost," Rachel hissed.
He was zooming around between the
stars. "Are you ready?"

Kirsty nodded. "Ready," she said.

The girls flew toward Jack Frost.

"Back again, girls?" he taunted,
when he spotted them. "Well, you'll
never get past me!"

"We're not scared of you!" Rachel called out loudly. "You're full of hot air, Jack Frost!"

Jack Frost gave a gleeful cackle. "Did you say hot air?" he asked. "This should cool you down!" He stretched out a bony finger. Bolts of magic ice lightning shot from his hand and flew straight toward Kirsty and Rachel!

Danger in the Stars

Kirsty and Rachel swerved aside in alarm! The lightning bolts thudded into the Twisty Tree behind them with a crash.

Rachel's heart pounded in fear, but she was not going to give up. "We have to keep him distracted," she muttered. "Come on, Kirsty!"

The girls bravely flew on toward Jack Frost.

"Haven't you learned your lesson?" he cried.

Another lightning bolt zigzagged toward the girls. They both veered away and it, too, whacked into the tree, knocking off a branch. Kirsty gulped. The ice lightning had come so close to her, she had felt it whistle past her wings.

But again, she and Rachel turned back
to face their enemy. And then, to her
delight, Kirsty saw Pegasus galloping
through the night sky behind Jack Frost!
As they got closer to the
diamond, Lucy clung
to Pegasus's silvery
mane. Kirsty heard
Rachel gasp with
excitement
and realized
that she had
also seen the
Diamond Fairy.
Now the girls
had to make sure
Jack Frost didn't
take his eyes off them

for a second, or else he might spot Lucy and Pegasus!

"Missed us," Kirsty called out. "You need to get your eyes tested, Jack Frost. You're not throwing straight!"

Jack Frost let out a thunderous roar of rage. "That does it!" he bellowed. "This time, I'll knock you pesky girls out of the sky!"

 But just as he started muttering a spell, Kirsty saw that behind him Pegasus and Lucy had reached the diamond. Lucy plucked it out of the sky and gave the girls a thumbs-up sign. Then Pegasus

soared away, his wings beating
powerfully.

Jack Frost heard the sound of Pegasus's
wings and broke off his spell. "What's
that?" he cried. He
turned and let out
an angry yell as
he spotted Lucy
on the winged horse.
He had been tricked!
"Come back!" he
roared, pointing his
wand at Pegasus.

The magical
horse neighed and
tossed his head as
a freezing bolt of
lightning hurtled toward him. Pegasus
dodged the bolt but had to swerve so

sharply that Lucy almost slipped off. She
clutched at his mane to keep herself
from falling. As she did, she lost her grip
on the diamond! Rachel and Kirsty
watched in horror as the jewel tumbled
through the air.

"I'll get it!" Kirsty yelled, diving toward the diamond as it fell. She flung out a hand, stretching to reach the jewel. "Yes!" she cried as her fingers closed around the diamond. "Got it!"

Jack Frost snarled. "Oh, no you don't!" he shouted, before calling out a spell.

Kirsty gasped as she felt her wings freeze and go numb. Jack Frost's spell had turned them to ice. She couldn't fly!

45

"Help!" Kirsty screamed, trying desperately to flap her icy wings. But it was no use — they were frozen solid. She kept falling, still clutching the diamond in her hand.

"Hold on, I'm coming!" Rachel cried, swooping toward her friend as fast as she could fly.

Jack Frost pointed his wand at Rachel, too, and a flood of icy sparkles shot toward her. But Rachel managed to dodge his magic and kept zooming after Kirsty at top speed. She finally reached her friend and grabbed Kirsty's hand. She flapped her wings as hard as she could, trying to drag her friend upward, but it was hopeless. Rachel's wings just weren't strong enough to carry two fairies. She found

herself and Kirsty sinking faster and faster toward the ground.

Jack Frost laughed nastily. Rachel thought that she and Kirsty were doomed to crash! But suddenly, Lucy and Pegasus were there, swooping beneath the girls.

Rachel and Kirsty landed on the horse's back with a jolt.

"Oh, thank you, Pegasus!" Kirsty gasped in relief. "And I still have the diamond!" she added.

"Take us to the royal palace, Pegasus," Lucy urged.

Just then, Rachel felt an icy blast behind her. She turned to see Jack Frost chasing after them on a gust of wind.

"Quick, Pegasus!" she cried. "Fly as fast as you can!"

Jack Frost was closing in on them, but Pegasus surged through the cloud layer. Soon, they had reached the warmer skies over Fairyland. Kirsty peered down and saw the royal palace below. King Oberon, Queen Titania, and the six other Jewel Fairies were waiting in the courtyard.

"Hold out the diamond, Kirsty," Lucy called. As Kirsty stretched out her hand, Lucy touched the end of her wand to the magic jewel. The diamond vanished in a fountain of sparks. But as Pegasus landed and the three friends slid down from his back, it reappeared, shining like a star in Queen Titania's crown.

Magic in every color of the rainbow sparkled around the Fairy Queen. She smiled at Kirsty and Rachel.

"Wonderful job, girls," she called in her soft, musical voice as she undid the spell on Kirsty's wings.

But at that moment, a terrible howl of rage echoed through the air. It was Jack Frost! He had followed Pegasus through the clouds and was hovering in the sky

overhead. "You girls have ruined everything!" he thundered. Then he waved his wand in a complicated pattern.

Instantly, the air turned bitterly cold. An icy wind sprang up and chased away the clouds. Above, the Fairyland stars seemed to tremble.

Kirsty looked up and cried out in fear. Showers of glittering, razor-sharp icicles were raining down on her and Rachel!

Fire and Ice

Quickly, Queen Titania lifted her own wand. Magic crackled from the tip in golden sparks. As the fiery sparks touched the icicles, the ice was transformed into rainbow-colored sparkles that drifted down harmlessly around the girls.

"NOOO!" Jack Frost shouted. He swung his wand toward the queen. At once, an icy wind rushed at her.

Queen Titania's wand flashed in the sky as the Fairy Queen cast another spell and sent a stream of rainbow-colored magic shooting toward Jack Frost. While the girls watched, the queen's magic collided with the icy wind. There was a huge explosion, and the night sky lit up with streaks of rainbow colors.

"It's like fireworks!"
Rachel gasped.

"And look,
Queen Titania's
spell is stronger
than Jack Frost's!"
Kirsty cheered. The
girls watched as
the queen's spell
forced Jack
Frost's ice-white
magic back
at him.

Jack Frost shouted in rage as he was
sent tumbling through the night sky by
his own icy spell. The girls watched him
grow smaller and smaller as he spun off
into the distance.

"That should keep him out of trouble
for a while," the queen said with
satisfaction. Then she turned to Rachel
and Kirsty. "My dear girls," she went on,
taking their hands. "You've saved
Fairyland again — and with such a
daring rescue! I can't tell you how
wonderful it is to have all the jewels back
in my crown again."

"You were amazing," Lucy added, hugging the girls. Then the six other Jewel Fairies rushed over to thank Kirsty and Rachel, too.

"Now it's time to recharge everybody's magic supply!" the queen announced. "Kirsty and Rachel will be our very special guests for the ceremony," she added. "Take your places please, fairies."

Kirsty and Rachel watched as the royal band, including their old friend, Bertram the frog footman, came out of the palace and began to play. At once, fairies came from all directions, laughing and cheering as they lined up behind the king and queen.

The queen motioned for Rachel and Kirsty to join her as she and the king led the procession into the palace.

"This is so exciting," Kirsty breathed as they marched through the Great Hall. "I hope it isn't just a nice dream that India has sent me!"

The procession entered a small room. The girls held their breath as the queen took off her crown and placed it

on a red velvet
cushion. Instantly,
a fountain of
sparkling light shot
up from each jewel.
The beams of light
met in midair
above the crown,
and formed a
twinkling rainbow of fairy dust.

"Wow!" Rachel exclaimed. "It's
so beautiful!"

The king and queen dipped their
wands into the rainbow, and the tips
glowed brightly. Then Lucy did the same,
and a faint outline of her wings reappeared
on her back. It grew brighter and
stronger until her wings shimmered and
shone with pure, sparkling fairy magic.

61

One by one, every
fairy in the
procession did
the same,
recharging each
wand with the
power of the jewels'
magic. And as their
wings reappeared, each fairy's face lit up
with happiness. "Look!" Kirsty said,
nudging Rachel. The two girls peeked out
of the window to see the courtyard
outside the palace filled with happy
fairies, fluttering and flying in circles just
for fun.

When all the fairies had recharged their
wands, the king and queen led Rachel
and Kirsty out into the courtyard, too.
There was so much magic in the air, it

was filled with sparks from all the fairy wands.

"Thank you again for your hard work, girls," the king said, smiling. "We would like you to have these as a token of our thanks." He handed each girl a beautiful ring.

"Oh, thank you," Rachel said, slipping the ring onto her finger. It fit perfectly, of course! "Look, Kirsty, in the rings are all the gems of Queen Titania's crown: moonstone, garnet, emerald, topaz, amethyst, sapphire, and diamond!"

"Every time I wear this ring, I'll remember the adventures we've had with the Jewel Fairies," Kirsty said. Then the queen touched her wand to each of the girls' golden lockets. "I refilled your lockets with fairy dust," she said. "You can come and find us if ever you need our help." She hugged both girls warmly. "And now, it's time for you to go home."

"Thank you for everything," Rachel and Kirsty called. The king waved his wand in the air and a haze of rainbow sparkles swirled around them. At once, the fairies' laughter faded and Rachel and Kirsty found themselves back in Rachel's bedroom.

"Oh, Kirsty," Rachel cried, gazing at her fairy ring. "What an adventure!"

Kirsty nodded, but before she could speak, there was a knock at the front door.

"We're just in time! My mom and dad must be here," Kirsty said, tucking her fairy ring safely into her bag.

"What an incredible week!" Rachel said, sighing. "I can't wait until our next visit."

Kirsty nodded happily. "Who knows what fairy adventures we'll have then!"

The two friends grinned at each other and hurried downstairs to the front door.

RAINBOW magic™

Rachel and Kirsty's fairy adventures
aren't over! Look for
The Pet Fairies
in March 2008!

Here's a special sneak peek at
Pet Fairies #1:

Katie the
Kitten Fairy!

A Very Unusual Kitten

"Catch!"

Kirsty Tate tossed a baseball into the air. She watched as her friend Rachel Walker ran across the grass to catch it. It was the first day of spring vacation and Rachel had come to stay with Kirsty's family for a whole week. The two girls were playing in the park while Kirsty's parents were out at the grocery store. The sun was shining brightly and there wasn't a cloud in the sky. It felt like perfect spring weather.

Rachel held up the ball triumphantly. "Your turn," she called. "Ready?"

Before Kirsty could reply, loud barking rang through the air. Both girls spun around to see a large black dog bounding past them.

Rachel jumped back as the dog raced by. "Is that a squirrel it's chasing?" she asked, watching the dog run off.

Kirsty shielded her eyes from the sun to take a better look. "No, it's a kitten!" she exclaimed. Her eyes widened at the sight of a tiny white-and-gray kitten scrambling across the grass as fast as it could. "What's a kitten doing in the park?"

"I don't know — but that dog's about to catch it," Rachel said in alarm. "Come on!"

The two girls started to run after the animals. But they hadn't gotten very far before a sudden flash of bright light flickered through the air. A cloud of amber-colored sparkles swirled around the kitten. Seconds later, the kitten had vanished — and an enormous striped tiger had appeared in its place!

Fairyland is never far away!
Look for these other

books:

The Jewel Fairies

Special Editions

And coming soon...

The Pet Fairies

A fairy for every day!

The seven Rainbow Fairies are missing! Help rescue the fairies and bring the sparkle back to Fairyland.

When mean Jack Frost steals the Weather Fairies' magical feathers, the weather turns wacky. It's up to the Weather Fairies to fix it!

Jack Frost is causing trouble in Fairyland again! This time he's stolen the seven crown jewels. Without them, the magic in Fairyland is fading fast!

Look for The Pet Fairies— Coming soon!

■ SCHOLASTIC

www.scholastic.com

FAIR